SANTA ANA PUBLIC LIBRARY

A Note to Parents and Caregivers:

Read-it! Readers are for children who are just starting on the amazing road to reading. These beautiful books support both the acquisition of reading skills and the love of books.

The PURPLE LEVEL presents basic topics and objects using high frequency words and simple language patterns.

The RED LEVEL presents familiar topics using common words and repeating sentence patterns.

The BLUE LEVEL presents new ideas using a larger vocabulary and varied sentence structure.

The YELLOW LEVEL presents more challenging ideas, a broad vocabulary, and wide variety in sentence structure.

The GREEN LEVEL presents more complex ideas, an extended vocabulary range, and expanded language structures.

The ORANGE LEVEL presents a wide range of ideas and concepts using challenging vocabulary and complex language structures.

When sharing a book with your child, read in short stretches, pausing often to talk about the pictures. Have your child turn the pages and point to the pictures and familiar words. And be sure to reread favorite stories or parts of stories.

There is no right or wrong way to share books with children. Find time to read with your child, and pass on the legacy of literacy.

Adria F. Klein, Ph.D.
Professor Emeritus
California State University
San Bernardino, California

Editor: Christianne Jones
Designer: Amy Muehlenhardt
Page Production: Brandie Shoemaker
Creative Director: Keith Griffin
Editorial Director: Carol Jones
The illustrations in this book were created digitally.

Picture Window Books
5115 Excelsior Boulevard
Suite 232
Minneapolis, MN 55416
877-845-8392
www.picturewindowbooks.com

Printed in the United States of America.

Library of Congress Cataloging-in-Publication Data
Blackaby, Susan.
One up for Brad / by Susan Blackaby ; illustrated by Len Epstein.
p. cm. — (Read-it! readers)
Summary: Brad is angry that Sis has all new things while he must settle for old ones,
until he realizes he has something new that she does not.
ISBN-13: 978-1-4048-2418-8 (hardcover)
ISBN-10: 1-4048-2418-9 (hardcover)
[1. Sibling rivalry—Fiction. 2. Brothers and sisters—Fiction. 3. Babies—Fiction.]
I. Epstein, Len, ill. II. Title. III. Series.

PZ7.B5318One 2006
[E]—dc22   2006003391

One Up
for Brad

by Susan Blackaby
illustrated by Len Epstein

Special thanks to our advisers for their expertise:

Adria F. Klein, Ph.D.
Professor Emeritus, California State University
San Bernardino, California

Susan Kesselring, M.A.
Literacy Educator
Rosemount–Apple Valley–Eagan (Minnesota) School District

PiCTURE WiNDOW BOOKS
Minneapolis, Minnesota

Brad thinks Sis is a lucky duck.

Sis has a new purple room.

Brad has the same old blue room.

Sis has a new white crib.

Brad has the same old wooden bed.

Sis has a new blanket with a flower on it.

Brad has the same old blanket with a dinosaur on it.

Sis has new stuffed animals.

Brad has the same old trucks.

Sis has new books with colorful pictures.

14

Brad has the same old books
with ripped pages.

Brad is mad. Life is not fair!

Sis has brand new everything.

Brad has the same old stuff.

Then Brad grins. Brad is the
lucky duck.

Brad has something that Sis does not have. Brad has a little sister.

More *Read-it!* Readers

Bright pictures and fun stories help you practice your reading skills. Look for more books at your level.

Bears on Ice 1-4048-1577-5
The Bossy Rooster 1-4048-0051-4
The Camping Scare 1-4048-2405-7
Dust Bunnies 1-4048-1168-0
Emily's Pictures 1-4048-2409-X
Flying with Oliver 1-4048-1583-X
Frog Pajama Party 1-4048-1170-2
Galen's Camera 1-4048-1610-0
Jack's Party 1-4048-0060-3
Last in Line 1-4048-2415-4
The Lifeguard 1-4048-1584-8
Mike's Night-light 1-4048-1726-3
Nate the Dinosaur 1-4048-1728-X
The Playground Snake 1-4048-0556-7
Recycled! 1-4048-0068-9
Robin's New Glasses 1-4048-1587-2
The Sassy Monkey 1-4048-0058-1
The Treasure Map 1-4048-2416-2
Tuckerbean 1-4048-1591-0
What's Bugging Pamela? 1-4048-1189-3

Looking for a specific title or level? A complete list of *Read-it!* Readers is available on our Web site:
www.picturewindowbooks.com